Lin's
BACKPACK

**Written by
Helen Lester**

**Illustrated by
Lynn Munsinger**

 GoodYearBooks

This is Lin's backpack.
What is making it jump?

Is there a frog in Lin's backpack?

No.

Is there a rabbit in Lin's
backpack?

No.

Is there a kangaroo in Lin's backpack?

No.

Are there grasshoppers in Lin's backpack?

No! No! No!